MARVEL

Los Angeles · New York

CONTENTS

THE CASE OF THE MISSING FLERKEN

It was a beautiful day in Lower Manhattan. Carol Danvers was enjoying her usual morning routine—she grabbed the newspaper, flipped to the funny pages, poured herself a bowl of cereal, and reached over to pat Chewie's head, but Chewie wasn't there! Chewie is Carol's pet Flerken and looks just like a cat. "Chewie!" Carol called. "Breakfast time!"

But Chewie was nowhere to be found! *Is she hiding?* Carol thought. *Maybe she fell asleep between the couch cushions?* After searching her apartment, Carol began to worry. Maybe Chewie got out!

Carol felt worried. Where could Chewie have gone? Did someone . . . take her? Suddenly, she noticed the file on the table. Moonstone! Her old archnemesis had recently popped back up, and always had it out for Carol. In fact, Moonstone had disguised herself as Carol before, so maybe she'd tricked Chewie into leaving with her!

Carol changed into her Captain Marvel suit and prepared to go look for Moonstone—but more eyes were always helpful on a search. "Let's see who might be available," she said to herself.

Captain Marvel decided to call her pal James "Rhodey" Rhodes, otherwise known as War Machine. It seemed like forever since she last saw him, and they were due for a catch-up. She rocketed off to Avengers Tower, where War Machine was working. Even though she was on an important mission, she enjoyed the flight over to headquarters.

Rhodey was in a super boring meeting when Captain Marvel flew up to the top floor window to get his attention. "I need your help on a mission to rescue Chewie!" she told him.

"You sure she's not, you know, in your sweater drawer or something?" Rhodey asked. Captain Marvel shook her head. Moonstone had stolen Chewie—she was sure of it! Rhodey agreed to help, and they set off to solve the case of the missing Flerken.

Carol knew that Moonstone
would make it hard for her to find
Chewie. Moonstone wouldn't hide just anywhere, even if she was still
on Earth. War Machine looked around the top of Mount Everest while
Captain Marvel searched the bottom of the ocean.

They met up again in the Sahara, but neither of them found Chewie.

"Maybe she's not on Earth after all," Captain Marvel said.

"Space is big," War Machine commented, but Captain Marvel wasn't worried.

"I have lots of friends," she said.

The two heroes traveled to a bunch of different star systems and asked everyone if they had seen Chewie—but nobody knew anything about Moonstone kidnapping a cat (or Flerken) and nobody knew where Moonstone could be hiding.

Captain Marvel even asked the Guardians of the Galaxy.
"I'll tell ya everything I know. *If* you can beat me at Ping-Pong," Rocket
said. And Captain Marvel won!

"Okay, spill, Rocket!" Captain Marvel demanded. She was getting
anxious to find Chewie.

"Ha! I don't know nothin'!" Rocket confessed. "I don't even like
Flerkens. You think I woulda helped find one?!" Captain Marvel couldn't
believe it. She was back to square one.

Finally, Captain Marvel noticed a cluster of black holes in a relatively empty quadrant of the Milky Way galaxy. "Those weren't there before!" she exclaimed. "The only person I know who can create black holes like that is Moonstone."

"What are we waiting for?" Rhodey said.

Rhodey used his navigational skills to pilot them to Moonstone's lair hidden on an asteroid between the black holes. The heroes burst in and confronted Moonstone. "Where's my cat—I mean, Flerken?" Captain Marvel yelled. Moonstone leaped up and immediately lobbed a laser beam at her old enemy.

Rhodey managed to block the laser beam, but Captain Marvel was ready. She gathered her own energy and hurled it at Moonstone. Moonstone dodged the first hit, but soon Captain Marvel and Moonstone were each sending zaps of energy across the lair until, finally, two of the blasts met. . . .

BOOM! The two blasts of energy burst against each other and exploded, knocking everyone back.

"Why are you even here?" Moonstone yelled.

Captain Marvel showed her the picture of her pet. "You stole Chewie, and I want her back!"

Moonstone shook her head. "I didn't take Chewie. I'm lying low and trying to stay out of trouble."

"Chewie's not here," Rhodey said. "Let's head back to New York."

Captain Marvel was embarrassed—and sad. She really missed Chewie and had been sure she would find her with Moonstone. If she wasn't there, where on Earth could Chewie be? Captain Marvel and Rhodey flew back to Carol's apartment in New York.

"Did you check the sweater drawer?" Rhodey asked.

"Come on, Rhodey. I looked everywhere! Chewie isn't here."

"Just check one more time," Rhodey suggested.

"Chewie!" Carol exclaimed.

"You were right, Rhodey. Guess she was

here the whole time!" Sure enough, Chewie was snuggled up in Carol's

fuzziest sweater, perfectly content after a nice warm nap.

TOTAL SUPER HERO

Kamala Khan was totally a super hero.

Or maybe she was a sort-of super hero. A person with sort-of super-powers. Kamala thought that was probably more accurate.

Her friend Bruno kept telling her she was a real super hero, not a sort-of super hero. But it didn't feel real to her. Not yet.

It was still all too new.

Here's how it all started.

One night, when Kamala was still just a normal teen, she'd been down by the Jersey City waterfront when a strange mist started to roll in off the river. It was the Terrigen Mist—a gas that reveals when people have special genes. A mist that can activate super-powers.

When Kamala staggered out of the mist, something was different. *She* was different. She looked just like her hero, Captain Marvel! Pretty quickly, Kamala figured out what had happened. She was an Inhuman! She now had the power to change the shape of her body, her face—even her size.

Kamala realized that she needed a super hero identity. While she wanted to honor her all-time favorite hero by naming herself Ms. Marvel, she also wanted her own look. Inspired by clothing customs from her Muslim upbringing, she created her very own costume.

Now she was Ms. Marvel. Protector of Jersey City. Scourge of criminals, safe-keeper of corner stores.

Sort-of super hero.

So that's how Kamala Khan became Ms. Marvel. But what was Ms. Marvel doing on this particular night?

"Nothin'," Ms. Marvel muttered, looking around. A cricket chirped. A few buildings away, a baby was crying. It was late, and everyone was home. Nobody was committing any crimes. Ms. Marvel knew she should be happy about this. Peace and quiet was good!

But she had been kind of looking forward to using her new powers on some evildoers.

"Well, I guess I'm going home," Ms. Marvel said to herself.

CRASH! Two people barreled into the alley.

Ms. Marvel watched as they stood up and squared off. She gasped quietly—one of them was Carol Danvers herself! Captain Marvel!

And the other was . . .

"The Inventor?!" Ms. Marvel squeaked. She knew all about that guy! He was half man, half bird—and all bad.

Captain Marvel raised her fist. A yellow glow began to build around her hand. But before she could zap the Inventor, he raised a homemade-looking weapon. It fired a strange pulse of light at Captain Marvel.

The ray of pulsing light wrapped itself around Captain Marvel like a squirming octopus of energy.

"Gah!" she yelled, pawing at the tentacles of light. But she couldn't dislodge them.

Ms. Marvel was torn. Should she pursue the villain? Or should she help her hero? She made her decision, and leaped down into the alley, stretching her legs impossibly long to help control her fall.

The Inventor grinned and fled.

BOOM. The Inventor's energy field vaporized in a cloud of blinding yellow light. Captain Marvel staggered back—right into the dumpster.

Ms. Marvel couldn't believe THE Captain Marvel was right in front of her! Even covered in old burrito wrappers, she was *so cool*.

"You're Ms. Marvel, right?" Captain Marvel said.

Ms. Marvel was shocked. "You . . . you know who I am?"

"Of course!" Captain Marvel said. "The Avengers got a report that the Inventor has squirreled away a piece of a Wakandan ship, so we all spread out to find it—and I'm assigned to check out Jersey City. It's

The two Marvels took off running after the Inventor. As they ran, Ms. Marvel's thoughts were racing. What was the Inventor doing with Wakandan aerial tech? Where could he possibly be keeping it?

And then, suddenly, she had an idea.

There was a scrap yard about ten blocks to the south. It had a lot of old cars, parts of boats, even bits of airplanes in it. If the Inventor had stolen Wakandan tech, then maybe he was using it to power one of his junkyard inventions!

"Got any ideas?" Captain Marvel asked. "You know this area better than I do."

"The scrap yard," Ms. Marvel said with confidence. She pointed an elongated finger. "It's down this street."

"Brilliant!" Captain Marvel cried. Ms. Marvel lengthened her legs to keep up with Captain Marvel. Soon, they arrived at the scrap yard.

The Inventor was there. Boy, was he ever there. Ms. Marvel's eyes went wide when she saw him.

"Adorable," he said with a sneer, looking down at the two super heroes from his stolen perch. "I bet you think you can beat me. Me, a genius scientist in a jet of my own design, complete with Wakandan tech!"

He punched a button and half a dozen missiles shot toward Ms. Marvel and Captain Marvel.

"Embiggen!" Ms. Marvel yelled. Captain Marvel raised her fists. They were shimmering with unearthly power.

Thinking fast, Ms. Marvel grabbed a junked car out of a scrap heap and hurled it at the Inventor.

"Keep 'em coming!" Captain Marvel yelled to Ms. Marvel. "Distract him!"

Ms. Marvel picked up cars, dumpsters, I-beams—whatever she could find—and threw them at the Inventor. He steered clear of each one, but that meant he wasn't looking at Captain Marvel . . . who was glittering brighter and brighter.

BOOM! Captain Marvel released a blast of power that shorted out the ship entirely.

"No!" the Inventor cried, as his ship plummeted toward the ground. Ms. Marvel grabbed the ship out of the air with her embiggened hand and held it tight.

"Righteous!" Ms. Marvel said.

The Inventor squirmed and squealed, but he was stuck in the powerless ship.

And just like that, it was over. They'd defeated the Inventor together.

"I owe you one, Ms. Marvel," Captain Marvel said. Behind them, agents of S.H.I.E.L.D. were hauling the Inventor away. She had already called it in to the rest of the Avengers to let them know the tech had been secured. "T'Challa told me to thank you on his behalf."

It was all sinking in—she'd teamed up with Captain Marvel, and they'd been a great team! "Happy to help," she said, her eyes wide. "Let's do this again soon."

Captain Marvel smiled. "I look forward to it," she said. And she stuck out her hand.

Ms. Marvel shook it enthusiastically.

Without another word, Captain Marvel rocketed off into space.

Ms. Marvel stood there for a long time, watching the trail of light fade and vanish.

Captain Marvel had shaken her hand. Captain Marvel had treated her like a partner. She had even told her she'd saved the day.

Maybe . . . just maybe . . .

"I am a real super hero!" Ms. Marvel exclaimed.

Ms. Marvel. Protector of Jersey City.

Scourge of the Inventor and junkyard thieves everywhere.

Total super hero.

FINESSED

By night, Miles Morales and Gwen Stacy are the super heroes known as Spider-Man and Ghost Spider.

But by day, they are students, and sometimes that means homework. Today that homework includes visiting the art museum and writing about a piece of art that inspires them.

They decided to invite along their new friend Jeanne, who is their age but had just graduated from MIT, a college for super smart students. She had just moved to New York, so Miles and Gwen had taken her under their wings.

"What's with all the security guards?" Miles asked. The guards were everywhere, watching all of the patrons very closely.

"Haven't you heard?" Jeanne laughed. "There's a new thief in town named Finesse. She's been robbing museums and posting videos of it online. She says she's the fastest and most agile thief in town. She even challenged super heroes to try and catch her."

"Did she now?" Gwen said. She wanted to find out more about Finesse.

That night on patrol, Gwen and Miles watched Finesse's videos.
She really was amazing. She spun like Black Widow. She fought like
Hawkeye. She even threw a trash can lid like she was Captain America.
Gwen was sure she could do better. Gwen had never met a villain she
couldn't catch.

"Just let me get a shot at her!" Gwen growled. "I'll show her 'fast'
and 'agile.'"

All of a sudden, an alarm sounded. It was the same museum they
had visited that morning.

"Looks like you might get your shot," Miles said. They swung off to
investigate the alarm.

When they arrived, there was Finesse, carrying one of the priceless paintings from the new exhibit!

"Hold it right there!" Gwen yelled. "You're not getting away from us!"

Finesse smiled slyly. "I think you overestimate yourselves."

A man stepped silently out from behind a pillar. He was wearing a white costume with black spots on it.

"This is The Spot," Finesse explained. "He makes portals that help me make getaways."

The Spot threw one of the black spots from his own costume and it stuck to the wall.

"See you later, super losers," Finesse called as she jumped straight into the black spot and disappeared.

"Oh no you don't!" Gwen yelled, diving through the portal after Finesse.

Miles was left face-to-face with The Spot. "You wouldn't want to just give up, would you?" he asked. The Spot took another black spot off of his costume and walked toward Miles.

When Gwen came through the portal, she was on a rooftop. Finesse stood in front of her, grinning.

"Oh, is somebody finally going to give me a challenge?" Finesse laughed, throwing a punch at Gwen's midsection.

"I'm gonna give you a healthy dose of 'consequences for your actions,'" Gwen said as she dodged the punch by pulling a full front flip over Finesse. Now it was Gwen's turn. She shot her webs at Finesse.

But Finesse did something Gwen hadn't expected. She flipped exactly the way Gwen just had.

"Anything you can do, I can learn just by seeing you do it," Finesse teased, tripping Gwen from behind. "That's my power."

As for Miles, he was trying to keep from falling into spots. The Spot threw them on the floor beneath him, and into the wall where he tried to land. He even threw them right at Miles. How was he supposed to stop this guy if he couldn't even land?

Finally, Miles slingshot himself forward, kicking straight at The Spot's face, but his foot went right through! The black spot on The Spot's mask was a portal, too, Miles realized, but he was already falling into it!

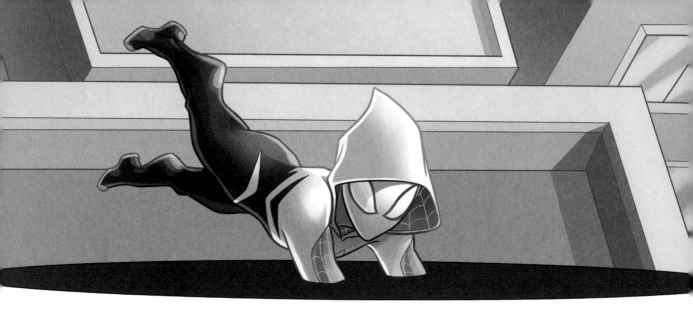

After popping in and out of roofs and walls, Gwen had lost sight of Finesse. She scanned the roof where she had popped out.

"I can't let her get away now!" Gwen grumbled. Then she saw it, another portal on the rooftop. That must have been where Finesse had gone! Gwen dove through headfirst.

And when she landed, she was in for a big surprise. A big, smelly, open dumpster waited for her.

"You too, huh?" came the voice from the dumpster next to her own. It was Miles, who had fallen through the portal in The Spot's mask and ended up here as well.

"I can't stand it!" Gwen yelled. "I almost had her! Next time I'm gonna catch her!"

"I know you want to prove you can beat her," Miles said, pulling a banana peel off his costume, "but if we're going to stop these thieves, we need a plan."

Miles and Gwen spent lunch the next day planning how they would handle things. When Finesse and The Spot tried to rob the museum the following day, they found Miles and Gwen waiting for them.

"Don't you know better than to steal ancient Egyptian artifacts, guys?" Miles quipped.

"Yeah, that's how you get attacked by mummies," Gwen added.

Finesse grinned again.

"Well, if you want it back, you'll

have to come and get it." With that, she ran for a nearby spot.

"She really gets on my nerves," Gwen grumbled.

"Stick to the plan," Miles urged.

"I am! Just . . . don't let her get away." With that, Gwen shot her

webline at The Spot and let Miles chase Finesse.

When Finesse
looked behind her,
there was nobody there. Had they just
decided to let her go? Why would they do that?
This was so strange that Finesse, not seeing
anybody chasing her, had stopped running just long
enough for Miles to catch up to her. He had used
his active camouflage to make himself invisible, and
Finesse couldn't taunt what she didn't see.

"Got you!" Miles reached out a hand and used his venom blast to
shock Finesse. She dropped the statue, and Miles snapped it up with
his hand.

Meanwhile, The Spot had a much harder time slowing down the agile Gwen. Each time he threw one of his spots, she webbed it up so she wouldn't fall through. She flipped, spun, and pirouetted away from The Spot.

The Spot got so frustrated that he tried to jump through one of his own portals and ended up tangled in one of Gwen's webs.

The next day, Gwen read the *Daily Bugle* headline to Miles: "'The Spot Captured in Historic Heist. Finesse Flees.'"

"You're upset, aren't you?" Miles asked. "I let her get away to save the statue."

"Are you kidding?" Gwen exclaimed. "It couldn't have gone better! I nabbed The Spot and I get another shot at Finesse. Next time—"

"Shhh," Miles cautioned as Jeanne sat down gingerly next to Gwen, holding her shoulder.

"Are you okay?" Miles asked Jeanne.

"Oh, I'm fine," Jeanne assured him. "I just messed up my shoulder last night. It won't happen again, though."

MARVEL
BLACK PANTHER
SHURI TO THE RESCUE

*W*HAM! Black Panther kicked a combat dummy so hard its head popped right off.

CRASH! The door slammed open. One of the *Dora Milaje*—Black Panther's most trusted warriors—ran in.

"Sire!" she said. "I am sorry to interrupt your training, but there is an emergency! Wakanda's national defense system is down!"

There was no time to lose. Black Panther strode out of the gym and hurried through the halls of his royal palace, giving orders.

"Get me my generals!" he commanded one of his aides.

"Get me my tech advisors!" he told another.

"Get me my—" he started.

"—sister?" a sly voice interrupted him.

"Yes, my sister!" T'Challa was happy to see Shuri, one of his smartest and most inventive scientists. As they made their way to the Wakanda command center, Shuri tried to offer advice, but Black Panther was busy directing his team. "Pull a report on all known super villain activity in sub-Saharan Africa," he told an aide.

"Find out if any of the border scouts have seen anything suspicious," Shuri told another aide.

"Run diagnostics on—" T'Challa started.

"—all activity leading up to the system failure," Shuri interrupted.

T'Challa stopped suddenly, eyeing his sister.

Shuri stared right back at her brother, determined. "I can help. I'm Wakanda's best technologist. The defense system going down is a technology failure. You need me."

One of the *Dora Milaje* spoke up. "This is more than a failure, sire. It appears to be a deliberate attack."

Shuri shrugged. "Then you need someone who is both a technologist *and* a warrior," she said. "Again: me."

Black Panther thought about it for a moment. She did have a point. He nodded. "Shuri," he said, "get your armor on."

Shuri grinned. "This is going to be fun!"

In Shuri's lab, T'Challa watched his sister in action. After several different tests and a thorough review of the diagnostics, it still wasn't clear why the system had shut down. Whoever was responsible for the failure was clever, but if anyone could figure out the problem, it was the Princess of Wakanda.

"We need to go to the auxiliary neural net in the Vibranium mound to access the system," she said. As soon as she started to put her armor on, Shuri realized that one of her gauntlets was missing! "So it wasn't just about the defense systems—that was a mere distraction to pull me from my lab!" Black Panther turned to issue an order to ready a jet, but Shuri beat him to it. "Face it, brother, this is my mission. And today, you are my sidekick."

Shuri piloted the quinjet through
Wakanda, but T'Challa wasn't ready for her
fast maneuvers! "Might as well have some fun
while we're at it," Shuri said with a laugh.

When they got to the auxiliary neural net, they saw an image of Doctor Doom's mask etched onto the side!

"Now what do we do?" T'Challa asked.

"Trust me, I can handle this," Shuri replied with confidence. "I have backup."

Shuri typed a few quick commands into her Kimoyo bracelet and within moments, Iron Man appeared!

"Tony?" T'Challa asked. "How do you know him?"

"He saw me give a talk on formal verification in quantum computing, and we've been corresponding ever since," Shuri said. "He sent me a message a few days ago because he heard Doctor Doom was working on something like my gauntlets. Tony's knowledge of tech—and Doctor Doom—may come in handy."

Iron Man radioed in to Shuri and told her to follow his lead. He knew exactly where Doctor Doom's secret lair was, so the three friends set off

As soon as the heroes arrived, Doctor Doom attacked. Doctor Doom managed to land a punch on Iron Man, but Black Panther was quick to fight back. Even with a single gauntlet, Shuri was a formidable warrior, and she sent a strong blast in Doctor Doom's direction.

The impact caught Doctor Doom off guard and knocked him back, causing Shuri's gauntlet to fall out of his cloak. "I was right! He was trying to re-create your tech," Iron Man said.

"There's not much to improve on, but I needed the gauntlet in order to make more of them!" Doctor Doom replied.

"Why go to all the effort of taking out our defense systems just to tell us it was you?" Shuri asked.

"And admit that you were just as smart as me? Never!"

Doctor Doom's
ego always was his
downfall. Tony hauled
Doctor Doom away,
but not before Shuri
promised to send Tony
her latest work on
microprocessor design.

Back at home in Wakanda, T'Challa thanked Shuri for her help. "I think of you as my annoying little sister," he admitted, "but you have become a most impressive young woman."

Shuri grinned. "And I think of you as my annoying big brother," she replied.

Black Panther waited for her to add a "but . . ."

She didn't.

"Bye, annoying big brother!" she said as she left. "See you next time the country needs saving!"

MARVEL
hawkeye

A TALE OF TWO HAWKEYES

Kate Bishop is not a morning person. Unfortunately, crime waits for no one, not even Kate. She may be a super hero, but even she can't bend the rules of time and space to sleep in longer.

"Morning, Hawkeye," says a voice from behind her.

"Morning, Hawkeye," Kate says through a mouth of Iron Bran.

Clint Barton—the other Hawkeye—joins her, holding two to-go cups.

"We're training today," he reminds her. "You ready to learn?"

"You sure you have anything left to teach me?" she teases.

"Oh, I still have a couple of tricks up my sleeve," he says. He hands her a cup.

When she takes it, it pops open—and a giant Doctor Doom puppet pops out!

Kate springs
into action,
defeating it with a
swift slap. She hates surprises, which Clint knows.

"Have to keep you on your toes, Hawkeye," he says, grinning.
"Part of your training."

Kate certainly won't let Clint get away with pranking her. If she has
to be ready for anything,
so does he.

It doesn't take Kate long to exact
her revenge. They meet at the gym later,
and Clint learns the hard way that Kate doesn't need super-powers to
stay a step ahead of the *old* Hawkeye.

When Clint goes to lift his barbell, it won't budge. He tries again.
And again, without success. He tries so hard he trips, and from his
spot on the ground, he sees that the weights are glued to the floor.

"Sorry, Clint," she says. "What you said about staying on your toes
really *stuck* with me."

Clint strikes back promptly. As soon as they move on to target practice, Clint takes the liberty of prepping Kate's arrows. As she's firing at the targets, nocking arrows at top speed, she reaches back and pulls out . . .

a rubber snake?!

She shrieks, dropping it.

The prank standoff continues.

As Kate and Clint bound across rooftops, Clint discovers that Kate's helping hand is *buzzzzzzzing* with ulterior motives.

Back at Hawkeye HQ, Kate prepares for a briefing on A.I.M.'s latest villain hijinks. As soon as she settles into her seat on the couch, though, the flatulent chorus of a whoopie cushion fills the room.

"The Fart of War," Clint says, and shrugs.

When they set the
pranks aside, though, Kate
and Clint train hard. They
take their jobs as heroes
seriously, and work to
make each other better.

Being a hero isn't just about fighting bad guys, though. The most important part of being a hero is being there for your community when it needs you. Even if someone in your community accidentally mistakes a raccoon for her cat stuck in a tree.

"Did you
do this?" Clint
asks after he's
returned to the ground.
"Because this is a next-level prank,
Hawkeye."

"Wish I could take credit, Hawkeye, but this one's just regular old
Clint Barton bad luck."

Kate and Clint keep a close eye on each other. As they stop crimes and help their neighbors during their evening patrol, they're on high alert, both ready for the next prank.

In her hyper-vigilance, Kate spots something to Clint's right: a figure, lurking in the alley. Clint radios the Avengers.

"A.I.M. was spotted in that area last week," Captain Marvel says. "Follow him."

Kate and Clint face off with A.I.M. Kate's holding her own in this big showdown as the rest of the Avengers arrive. She's worked hard and she's ready.

Together, the Avengers
defeat A.I.M.

"Well done, Hawkeye," Clint says.

"Thanks, Hawkeye." Kate grins.

Kate Bishop has put in the work to be at the top of her game. She trains hard, sharpens her skills, and is learning how to be part of a team. She also puts up with Clint, which is no easy task. Kate's ready for anything—including proving that she's the *best* Hawkeye.

MADE IN MAGIC

In Greenwich Village in New York City, Doctor Strange and Scarlet Witch were practicing their magic at the Sanctum Sanctorum, Doctor Strange's enchanted home. Scarlet Witch had asked him to help her practice her spells, and her Hex Bolts were growing stronger and stronger. She gathered energy in her hands and . . .

Doctor Strange dove to the side. Even with the help of his Cloak of
Levitation, he was barely able to fly out of the way fast enough.
The Hex Bolt exploded and his desk burst into flames!

"You're getting better," Doctor Strange told her. "All that power will come in handy one of these days."

"Thank you," Scarlet Witch replied. "Although I think we should be done with practice for the day. How about a coffee? It's on me."

As they walked toward the front door, Doctor Strange silently conjured a water spell. The flames on his desk were quickly snuffed out. "After you," he said.

The crisp fall air was the first thing Doctor Strange and Scarlet Witch noticed as they stepped outside Strange's magically protected home. The second thing they noticed was that every single person on the street was frozen in place.

"That's not exactly what you want to see," said Doctor Strange.

Doctor Strange looked over at his fellow Avenger. Scarlet Witch stood motionless. Her mouth hung slightly open. Her eyes were wide, yet she didn't blink. It was as if she was in a trance.

Suddenly, Doctor Strange felt a wave of terror rush over him.

He couldn't move either!

High above New York City, thunder boomed. Lightning flashed. The sky itself was tearing open to take the shape of a doorway. A figure flew through its opening. Doctor Strange recognized the figure instantly as one of his oldest foes: the ruler of the Dark Dimension, one of the most powerful sorcerers to ever live. Dormammu!

"As soon as you set foot outside your fabled Sanctum Sanctorum, my spell took hold," Dormammu said. He hovered in front of Scarlet Witch and Doctor Strange. "You were the last two on this planet to fall under the sway of my memory spell."

Doctor Strange was not listening to the words of his old enemy. Dormammu's spell had taken hold of him. Strange's mind was somewhere else. He was in the past, trapped in a memory.

It was years ago, back when Doctor Stephen Strange was a successful surgeon. All the money, success, and praise had gone to his head. He was selfish and thought that the rules didn't apply to him.

One night, while in his car, he was driving much too fast on a road that had too many turns. Doctor Strange's car shot off the cliff. There was a crash and an explosion. And then his world went black.

In his memory, Stephen Strange woke up to find that his days of being a surgeon were over. His hands had been damaged beyond repair.

But Doctor Strange refused to give up. He searched the world for a cure. What he found instead was something very different.

What he discovered was quite simply . . . magic.

After meeting a sorcerer called the Ancient One, Strange realized that the only way to fix his life wasn't to fix his hands. It was his attitude that needed work. His old life was over. It was time to think about others for a change.

But before he could act . . . before he could do anything at all, Doctor Strange was suddenly back in the hospital. He was a surgeon again.

The memory spell was starting over. He was trapped in its repeating loop!

Doctor Strange wasn't the only one stuck in a memory. Scarlet Witch was caught in Dormammu's spell as well. In her mind, she was back on Wundagore Mountain as a little girl named Wanda Maximoff. As she grew older, Wanda found she could tap into chaos magic and use powerful energy in bursts that she called Hex Bolts. Likewise, her twin brother, Pietro, discovered his own fantastic abilities. He could move at super speeds. No matter how much they wanted to have regular, ordinary lives, Wanda and Pietro were destined to be different.

Believing that she could offer no good to the world, Wanda and her brother, who adopted the name Quicksilver, joined forces with a team of villains.

When Scarlet Witch met the Avengers, she and her brother soon realized the error of their ways. The Avengers had also been gifted with special abilities, but they embraced those powers. They celebrated what made them different.

She was inspired by these heroes. But before she was able to remember when she became an Avenger herself, Wanda's thoughts looped back to Wundagore Mountain. She couldn't escape the spell.

Back in the real world, Dormammu was pleased. He had Earth's sorcerers exactly where he wanted them—and the dimension was finally his. But Dormammu didn't realize that the heroes' magical abilities were telling them that it wasn't real. Doctor Strange was remembering that he was no longer a selfish man—he was the Sorcerer Supreme! And Wanda was no longer a villain—she was an Avenger! They had changed the course of their lives for the better. They were heroes now.

An explosion of white-hot magic ripped through the air and knocked Dormammu off his feet. The two heroes had managed to release themselves from the memory loop and were fighting back!

Scarlet Witch fired a Hex Bolt at the villain before he realized what was happening. As she pushed Dormammu back, Doctor Strange opened a portal to a prison dimension behind Dormammu.

"Good-bye now," Scarlet Witch said. Before Dormammu could react, she shot another fiery Hex Bolt at him. It was her strongest yet. The evil sorcerer was forced backward into the dimension beyond the portal.

In a blinding flash of light, the portal—and Dormammu—vanished!

All along the street, people awoke from the trance. They shook
their heads and—without a second thought—continued on with their
day as if nothing had happened.

"See. Told you all that power would come in handy," Doctor
Strange said to Scarlet Witch.

Scarlet Witch laughed and then said, "So . . . same time tomorrow?"

"Of course," Doctor Strange replied. "Let's get that coffee before
practice tomorrow!"

Scarlet Witch looked forward to it.

SHIELDING FROM DANGER
PART ONE

The Winter Soldier's boots slipped just a little as they slushed into the wet snow on the rooftop. He adjusted his balance but didn't slow down. He was on patrol and was determined to find something interesting to do with his night. As he leaped to the neighboring roof of a warehouse, he heard a buzzing in his ear.

"Bucky? You there?"

It was Captain America's voice.

"Hey, Cap," answered Winter Soldier. He rolled as he landed on the warehouse's roof.

"GPS has you near the Manhattan Bridge," Captain America said over the Avengers comm device in Winter Soldier's ear.

"I always love it when you keep tabs on me," Winter Soldier said sarcastically. He and Captain America had been partners years ago, back when Winter Soldier was just a kid called Bucky Barnes. Now that he had grown up, Bucky couldn't resist giving his mentor a hard time now and again.

Cap didn't take the bait. Instead, he simply said, "There's a situation."

"You're about a block away from an inactive top secret S.H.I.E.L.D. base," Captain America continued. "There's been a break-in."

"Address?" Winter Soldier asked. Bucky didn't mind taking orders—as long as they were from Captain America.

"Underground at the corner of Morris and Second," said Cap. "The facility has been made to look like a standard construction site."

"Wow," Bucky said as he reached the site. He was impressed. "Now that's a disguise."

Bucky would never have guessed there was more to this building than steel beams and an elevator.

"The alarms went off on Sub-basement 2," said Cap. "They've been using the lab there to store a miniature force-field projector. I've just learned that Taskmaster is trying to get his hands on it. I'm on my way, but it'll take me a few minutes."

"Take your time," Winter Soldier whispered so he wouldn't be overheard. "I've been looking for some action tonight anyway."

Winter Soldier turned the volume on his comm unit down low. Then he held his breath for a second. He listened to his surroundings and scanned the high floor of the building with a few cautious glances. Then he moved carefully toward the elevator.

He placed the palm of his metal hand against a display panel by the elevator's doors. The screen flashed red. Bucky's fingers flexed. A pulse shot from his hand. The screen turned green.

Winter Soldier smiled. His metal arm had saved the day so many times on his missions. Tonight was proving to be no exception.

After a moment or two, the elevator doors opened with a *ding*.
Suddenly, a laser blast struck Winter Soldier! Luckily for Bucky, it

In front of him, two spinning drones shot off more laser blasts.
Winter Soldier jumped into the air. His fingers found the beam above
him, and he swung himself up. The drones hummed as they followed

As the first drone shot up toward him, sending a laser blast that narrowly missed his head, Bucky pounced and grabbed the drone tightly with both hands. It was like trying to hold on to a giant top, but he held on tight. His weight instantly pulled the drone down, crashing it into its companion and knocking it out of the air. Bucky swung toward the nearest beam. He took the drone with him and smashed it into a nearby support pillar. Sparks shot everywhere!

Bucky examined what little of the drone he still held in his hand. This wasn't S.H.I.E.L.D. technology. This belonged to someone else.

Suddenly, laughter echoed from inside the elevator.

"Sounds like an invitation," Winter Soldier muttered to himself. He stepped into the waiting elevator car, then pressed the button marked SUB-BASEMENT 2.

As the doors closed, Winter Soldier looked up. There was no escape hatch of any kind. He reached into a pouch on his belt.

The elevator car suddenly lurched. Then it lurched again. Winter Soldier understood what was happening right away. The elevator's cables were snapping one by one! Someone had damaged them.

He quickly tossed a small capsule up toward the ceiling of the car, shielding his face as the capsule exploded.

Bucky leaped for the newly formed hole above him just as the platform gave way beneath his feet. His metal hand reached out toward the wall of the elevator shaft as he tried to grab on to something . . . anything . . .

The car plummeted right past Bucky's intended floor and crashed on Sub-basement 3, and the force of the explosion shook the elevator shaft. Above the wreckage, a figure hovered on a circular glider.

The man's laughter filled the metal corridor. His helmet lit the room with its fluttering flame: Jack O'Lantern! He was having a great night.

His trap had worked perfectly. The second his drones had detected Winter Soldier, he had gotten to work damaging the elevator's cables.

Jack O'Lantern scanned the pile of rubble and steel through his strange flaming helmet.

"What are we looking for?" a voice asked from above him.

Jack O'Lantern glanced up just as one of Winter Soldier's boots struck his pumpkin head. Winter Soldier had been hiding above him in the elevator shaft. The force knocked Jack O'Lantern completely off his glider.

The villain hit the ground with a thud, fumbling for words. "How . . . how did you . . . ?" Too stunned to form a proper sentence, Jack raised his hand and pointed it at Winter Soldier. There was a clicking sound, but nothing else.

Jack O'Lantern's wrist blaster wouldn't fire. It had been damaged in his fall.

"Time to surrender, Pumpkin Spice," Bucky said with a wry grin.

Jack O'Lantern reached for one of the pumpkin bombs dangling from his belt. He tossed it at Winter Soldier.

Bucky swatted it away, as if it was nothing more than a fly.

The bomb exploded harmlessly against a nearby wall. Winter Soldier smiled wider.

And just like that, Jack O'Lantern wasn't laughing any longer.

It was quiet in Sub-basement 3 as Winter Soldier finished tying Jack O'Lantern's restraints.

Suddenly, Bucky's comm unit broke the silence.

"I'm almost there," said the voice of Captain America in his ear. The voice was muffled. There wasn't much reception so far underground.

"You missed the party," Winter Soldier said. "I nabbed Jack O'Lantern here, but I think we still have a problem."

"What's going on?" Cap asked.

"There's no sign of the force-field projector," said Winter Soldier. "I even checked inside this guy's giant gourd," he continued, smiling down at Jack O'Lantern. The criminal only grunted. "I'll look in the lab next, but—"

Before Winter Soldier could finish his thought, the call dropped. Just then, Bucky heard a rustling of something like wings in the shadows behind him.

"It's worse than you think," a mysterious voice said.

Winter Soldier tightened his fists.

The night was finally getting interesting.

To be continued . . .

SHIELDING FROM DANGER
PART TWO

A figure hovered in the darkness above Winter Soldier. The lights in the hallway of the S.H.I.E.L.D. facility had been damaged, causing a flicker that made it hard to see. Bucky steeled himself for battle. Then the man swooped down into the light, his boots padding silently against the metal floor as he landed.

"We need to move fast," said Falcon, leaving the shadows behind.

"This way," said Falcon. He sprinted toward the stairwell. Without hesitation, Bucky followed.

As they raced to the laboratory one floor up, Falcon filled Bucky in on what had happened. He felt like he was missing something. Something important . . .

Falcon had been flying home earlier that evening, ready to turn in. It had been a particularly tiring night of patrol, and Sam Wilson was doing his best to relax and enjoy the rest of the night. The fresh snow falling in the crisp air made that a little easier for him.

That's when he saw the dark cloud moving toward him. At first, Falcon couldn't understand what he was seeing. The cloud was swirling and swaying, as if pulsing with life. As he flew closer, Falcon realized it wasn't a cloud at all. It was a swarm of bats!

Falcon did his best to use his wings as a shield against the sudden swarm. Fortunately, the bats weren't all that interested in him. They seemed to have another target in mind.

Falcon watched to see where they were heading. As if with a single mind, the bats dove toward a nearby construction site.

"What in the world?" Falcon said under his breath. Then he put his wings to his sides and dove to follow.

As he closed in on the bats, Falcon could see that they were flying straight toward an elevator at the center of the abandoned site. The doors to the shaft were open, as if expecting the winged creatures. Falcon clenched his jaw and dove faster.

He swooped into the empty elevator shaft after the bats. The doors were closing, but Falcon managed to make it through before they slammed shut.

Falcon felt like he was diving forever as his eyes adjusted to the dark elevator shaft. He realized that he and the bats must be far underground by this point. This empty construction site wasn't what it appeared to be.

Finally, the bats exited through the open doors of a floor marked Sub-basement 2. Falcon slowed his speed and landed just outside the elevator. The hallway was completely deserted.

The corridor was lined with glossy metal walls and thick steel doors that were locked tight. High-tech security cameras were mounted on the ceiling, each with a broken lens. Falcon recognized the technology right away. This was a S.H.I.E.L.D. base.

The hallway stretched out in front of the hero. Falcon could see the flutter of wings near its end, and what seemed to be the light of an open door. He hadn't taken more than a few steps forward when two bat-shaped throwing stars shot into his wing. Falcon had no time to react. Suddenly, a much larger bat was headed straight for him!

As Falcon bent backward to dodge the speeding "bat," he realized what he was actually facing. It was a glider, one used by a villain he and Captain America had faced many times in the past. A criminal who just happened to be able to control bats.

"When I called for reinforcements, I wasn't expecting anyone human," said a voice from down the corridor.

Falcon's suspicions had been confirmed. "Blackwing," Sam said, as the villain's glider crashed into the wall behind him.

Blackwing reached into his cape and pulled out a battle baton. Without another word, he charged at the hero, his bats leading the way.

Falcon took to the air. There wasn't much room to move around in the tight corridor, but he wasn't in the mood for anything fancy, anyway. Falcon simply flew directly at Blackwing.

Falcon pierced the cloud of bats like a javelin hurtling toward its target. Blackwing's eyes widened as he saw this bullet of a man heading straight for him. The villain tried to dodge the hero, but it was too late. Blackwing was knocked backward, through the open doorway at the end of the hall and into a glass countertop in the high-tech S.H.I.E.L.D. laboratory.

Sam was still in motion and flipped forward off the villain.

He was instantly back on his feet.

Blackwing wasn't as graceful. He lay on the ground in a pile of broken computer components. He tried to speak but let out a pitiful groan instead. Then he was completely unconscious.

"And this is where I left him," Falcon said. He and Winter Soldier had just burst into that same S.H.I.E.L.D. laboratory on Sub-basement 2. They had made the sprint from the lower floor in seconds.

"You were talking over your comm link earlier about a force-field projector," said Falcon. "I've seen prototypes before, but this guy didn't have anything like that on him." He nodded at Blackwing, lying in a lump in the middle of the room. "Only thing that stood out to me was that empty safe."

"So Jack O'Lantern and Blackwing . . ." said Winter Soldier. "They were just cover?" He bent down and picked up Blackwing's battle baton.

"That's what I'm thinking," said Falcon. "Low-level henchmen to keep

"Comm's down," said Winter Soldier, tapping his ear. "Cap's on his way, but I don't know when—"

"Wait," interrupted Falcon. "Over there." He pointed to a lone bat, flapping in the corner of the lab. The confused creature flew into the hallway, but in the opposite direction of the elevator shaft. "I think there's another way out of here," said Falcon.

Falcon leaped into the air, and Winter Soldier raced after him. They followed the bat into a long, empty tunnel.

Near the end of the tunnel stood a figure dressed in orange and blue. As he turned to face the heroes, Falcon instantly recognized him. It was Taskmaster! He was a villain more dangerous than Blackwing and Jack O'Lantern combined.

In one hand, Taskmaster clutched a shield, similar to that of Captain America. In the other, he held a small device about the size of a remote control. Falcon realized the device Taskmaster was holding was S.H.I.E.L.D.'s missing force-field projector.

"Knew I should've hired more guys," said Taskmaster.

Without taking his eyes off the villain, Falcon spoke to Winter Soldier under his breath. "Go for the button."

Winter Soldier narrowed his eyes. He had worked with Falcon enough times to know exactly what he meant.

As Taskmaster readied his shield to hurl it at the heroes, Winter Soldier threw Blackwing's battle baton.

Winter Soldier had always been an expert marksman. This throw was no exception. Blackwing's battle baton hit the button on the projector just as Falcon flew full speed at Taskmaster. The two heroes had worked with Captain America enough to know what to expect—Bucky went low while Falcon went high.

Taskmaster didn't think twice. He simply launched the shield at the oncoming Falcon. If he had used that second thought, Taskmaster might have realized that the force-field projector had been switched on. But as it was, the shield ricocheted off of the protective energy field and was reflected right back at him. The blast stunned the villain just as Falcon tackled him off his feet.

The force-field projector fell out of Taskmaster's hand and slid across the floor.

The projector came to a stop at Captain America's boots.

"Guess you didn't need my help," said Cap as he picked up the device. He pressed the main button on the projector. The force field around Taskmaster instantly shut down.

The villain put his gun on the floor and raised his hands in a gesture of surrender.

"What, you think you're the only Captain America in town?" Winter Soldier said, grinning at Cap. He patted Falcon on the back, and Falcon grinned, too.

The heroes pulled Taskmaster to his feet and began walking him back toward the S.H.I.E.L.D. base. The lights of the hallway were bright above them, but there was hardly a shadow in sight.

ENEMY NUMBER ONE

Hello. I know this book has a lot of stories in it, but this is the only one you really need. It is, after all, about the greatest hero of all time. Me! Loki!

What story should I tell you? I have so many good ones. There's the time I humiliated Thor. The time I beat all of the Avengers. Maybe the time I beat up the Hulk?

Wait, I know—what's a good hero without a great enemy? I'll tell you the story of my greatest foe. A real dastardly villain.

Once upon a time, giant wolves with terrible teeth and claws like knives attacked the lands outside of Asgard. Things had gotten so bad that a group of Asgard's greatest hunters were gathering to go out and hunt the wolves. My brother, Thor, being more brave than bright, wanted to join them, but they told him he was too young.

"You're the Prince of Asgard," I told him. "You don't need their permission. Let's go together, brother, and win the glory for ourselves." Thor agreed, and so we went.

On the way, I had the best idea for a prank. I replaced Thor's sword with a trick sword that would break as soon as he started fighting. The wolves would almost certainly eat him. It should have been a great joke.

Then she had to come along and ruin everything. We found this farm girl with long blond hair fighting the wolves with a stick. Of course, Thor just had to help her.

My plan worked perfectly. As soon as Thor hit one of the wolves with his sword, the whole blade shattered. He would have been helpless!

Except here came that girl with her stick. First she defended him, then they started working together! Thor asked me to help, so I had to pretend. I threw a fireball that went sailing off into the sky, nowhere near the wolves.

Imagine my surprise when the hunters from Asgard saw it and came to save us. Oh joy.

I was annoyed, but at least I would never see this farm girl again, right? WRONG! The next month she shows up in Asgard. It turns out she's actually a lady of Asgard and as she was such a good fighter, she had decided to come train. Her name was Sif, and she was the worst.

To make matters worse, Thor wouldn't stop talking about her. It was always "Sif this" or "flowing golden locks that." The only thing more obnoxious than my brother Thor is my brother Thor in love. Gross.

Thor and Sif started hanging out all the time. Pretty soon she was putting ideas in his head.

"I'm sure Loki has your best interests in mind, Thor, but roasting marshmallows on Surtur sounds dangerous. Wouldn't you rather spar with me?"

She was doing it on purpose! She was interfering with all my plans! I had to find a way to make her stop.

Being the genius I am, I had the perfect plan. In the middle of the night, I would use magic to steal every strand of that beautiful golden hair Thor loved so much, then I'd sneak away. Neither Sif nor Thor would ever suspect me. Once Thor stopped spending all his time with her, I could go back to trying to maroon him with frost giants.

It almost worked, too.

On the way out, I must have made a noise, because all I heard was a roar like a wild animal, and Sif catapulted across the room in no time.

She tackled me in the middle of the room. I was so surprised I couldn't even defend myself. She pinned me down and started yelling, "Why did you do this? I've been nothing but nice to you!" Her voice was earsplitting.

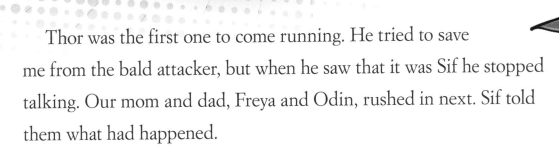

Thor was the first one to come running. He tried to save
me from the bald attacker, but when he saw that it was Sif he stopped
talking. Our mom and dad, Freya and Odin, rushed in next. Sif told
them what had happened.

"I can replace it," I yelled, hoping that would get her off of me.

"Very well," said Odin. "You have one day to replace Sif's hair or I
shall grant her her revenge."

Thing is, making something *reappear* is a lot harder than making it
disappear.

I didn't know where one could get a head full of hair, so I figured I'd try the dwarves of Nidavellir. Dwarves can make anything.

They're also very rude. I tried all of the top smiths, and they all said they were too busy to work with a trickster. So I took one last shot at the dwarf I knew was the second-best smith. At first, he refused, until I said: "You know, I heard you were the second-best smith. I know what that's like. I've been Odin's second-best son my whole life. Maybe, if we work together, we can both be the best today."

That got his attention. He started working right away.

Wouldn't you know it, a few hours later he had made a crown with a head full of blond hair. He handed it to me, saying, "All you need to do is place this on their head and they'll have a full head of blond hair again. Now, about my payment."

"I didn't say anything about payment."
I laughed, snapped my fingers, and disappeared. What a chump!

When I got home, I called for a little ceremony so that all of the gods could appreciate my genius and see Sif's shiny head.

I placed the beautiful crown on Sif's head, saying "I, Loki, Prince of Asgard and God of Mischief, humbly apologize to you, Lady Sif, for taking your hair. To make amends, I replace it with this finely crafted crown and hair."

Unfortunately, the dwarven smith had enchanted the crown, knowing that I might betray him. Since I had not paid, Sif's golden locks turned raven black. Honestly, I thought she looked better this way. I've always been partial to dark hair.

She was not so happy and tried to stab me, but Odin stopped her.

"Loki swore he would replace your hair, and he has. There was no promise made about the color of the hair," Odin's voice boomed.

She couldn't stab me, but Sif pulled me close and said, "I'll see to it that you're never trusted again! No matter what you do, I'll stop you."

So, if you've read this far, you probably already guessed who my greatest villain is. Who did you guess?

That's right! It's me! I'm my own worst enemy. I learned that day that if you're going to play pranks, you shouldn't break anything you can't fix. A good trickster always needs to think two steps ahead.

I mean, who else could even compare? Sif? Ha! Like I'd be afraid of that grumpy, perfectionist, Thor-loving . . .

Whoops, she's right behind me, isn't she? Now I'm in for it.

MARVEL

THE MIGHTY THOR

BECOMING THE MIGHTY THOR

Jane Foster had always felt that helping people was her calling. Her hope was to heal the pain and suffering of others, so she became a doctor.

She took great care in treating her patients, and they trusted her. She wasn't just good at her job. She went to extra lengths to comfort everyone she treated with kindness and a gentle heart.

But like her patients, Jane was also sick. Her good friend Thor admired her for helping others, but he was still worried about her.

"You look tired, Jane. You need to take care of yourself and get some rest," he told her.

"I know, but I also want to take care of the people who need me," Jane replied. "I can do both."

"I understand," Thor said. "I feel the same sense of duty as a part of the Avengers."

Jane had always wanted to meet them, so Thor took her to Avengers Tower and introduced her to the team. Jane was moved by their dedication to fighting against injustice, and captivated by their fierce warrior abilities. Each member of the Avengers brought a different skill set to the group.

"Together, we are united by a common goal—to protect and defend Earth and other realms of the universe from evil," Thor explained.

Thor's sense of duty never changed, but one day he discovered that he was unable to lift his hammer, Mjolnir. He had become unworthy. He knew that he still had battles to fight, so he began to use Jarnbjorn—a weapon forged by the dwarves that he had used long before Mjolnir.

So Mjolnir found someone else who was worthy.

Jane heard Mjolnir calling to her. One minute, she was in bed being summoned. The next, she was flying through the stars to the moon!

Whosoever holds this hammer, if they be worthy, shall possess the power of . . .

Thor

Mjolnir lay in wait on the moon, gleaming with light and hope. The hammer had been cast from a mystical Asgardian metal that came from the heart of a dying star.

"I can feel it pulling me toward it," Jane said to herself. Without hesitation, she effortlessly picked it up and lifted it into the air.

As soon as she raised the hammer, a massive force of energy took hold of her whole body. She held tightly to Mjolnir and felt herself transforming into something powerful . . . something superhuman. . . .

While Jane had already been worthy of wielding the hammer, she now *felt* worthy.

Finally, it all made sense—her need to help people, meeting Thor and the Avengers, and now being called by Mjolnir.

It was her destiny. She had become The Mighty Thor!

Jane used the power from Mjolnir to act as a brave warrior. She embraced her calling with honor by helping wherever she could.

And sometimes that meant battling evil beings like Loki! He had
stolen a mystical, glowing purple stone, and Black Widow was there to
help The Mighty Thor get it back.

"That's not your hammer," Loki told Jane.

"Mjolnir says otherwise," she retorted, "but that's definitely not
your artifact." As Jane lunged for the stone, Loki quickly conjured a
protective energy shield around himself.

Jane raised her hammer. As thunder boomed and lightning flashed, she sent a massive energy blast at Loki, shattering his protective shield. Loki fell to the ground, caught off guard, and the stone rolled out of his hand.

"Got it!" exclaimed Black Widow.

"Tsk, tsk," Jane scolded Loki. "You should know better than to take things that don't belong to you."

Over time, Jane went on more and more missions. Sometimes she teamed up with the Avengers, and other times she worked on her own.

She knew that Mjolnir had chosen her for a reason. As a doctor, she'd had a calling to help people. As a super hero, she had the power and duty to protect all beings.

But for Jane, being a hero wasn't just about having super-powers or being chosen.

It was about purpose. It was about helping wherever she was needed, no matter what. Jane fought with strength and courage, acted out of humility, and led with honor. After all, she had not only a calling but a destiny to fulfill.

Jane was The Mighty Thor!

MARVEL
SHANG-CHI

SHADOWS OF THE SON

Shang-Chi lived in Chinatown in San Francisco. He worked at Wang Bakery, which sold pineapple buns and other delicious, sweet treats. People went there to see Shang-Chi's quick moves as much as they went for the food. Shang-Chi enjoyed showing off his skills at the bakery, but he kept his real talents hidden away from his day-to-day customers.

In truth, Shang-Chi was much more than a part-time assistant at a bakery. Shang-Chi was a master of martial arts! When not stopping purse-snatchers or saving the world from super villains, he was busy fighting a secret war that had started long ago.

Shang-Chi grew up in a remote temple in China and lived far removed from the modern world. In fact, he was raised as if he were living in the ancient Qing Dynasty! Modern technology was simply not the way of his father, Zheng Zu.

Zheng Zu was a cruel man. He never laughed. He rarely even smiled. But, nonetheless, he was respected by many people. Other lost souls followed him, embracing an era that had long passed.

Zheng Zu taught Shang-Chi and his sister, Shi-Hua, ancient forms of martial arts.

Both desperately wanted their father's approval. But instead, they had to settle for his harsh words and constant criticism.

Zheng Zu was the head of five schools of fighting. The schools were spread around the world, but Zheng Zu made sure they all met his high expectations. Each school was named after a weapon: Hand, Hammer, Sabre, Dagger, and Staff. And each school had its chosen champion!

In China, Shang-Chi's hard work and dedication paid off and he became the Champion of the Hand. In fact, his skill and mastery of the martial arts began to rival Zheng Zu's!

In Russia, Shi-Hua studied and trained hard, too. She became the Champion of the Hammer and took on a new name to reflect her accomplishments: Sister Hammer.

All through those years, Zheng Zu never told Shang-Chi the whole truth about who he really was. One day, when Shang-Chi was supposed to be practicing, he spied on his father. He found out that his father had mastered a form of dark magic and was planning to use it to take over the world.

Shang-Chi had been sheltered from the real world for his entire life, but he knew evil when he saw it. He knew he had to stop his father, so he confronted Zheng Zu.

It took every ounce of energy and every bit of skill Shang-Chi could muster, but he stopped his father and put an end to the cruelty.

Shang-Chi decided to travel to America. He didn't want to be like his father, so, instead, he became a super hero! Shang-Chi joined the Avengers. Together, they fought evil threats that no single hero could defeat alone.

The people of San Francisco saw Shang-Chi as a humble clerk at a bakery, but there was much more to him than that. Shang-Chi had made it his life's mission to protect the world, and nothing would stop him from helping people.

FRIENDLY NEIGHBORHOOD SUPER HERO!

Peter Parker lived in a house in Queens, New York, with his Aunt May. Aunt May raised Peter as if he were her own son. She was very nurturing and made sure he had everything he needed. Before his Uncle Ben passed away, he told Peter he could become whoever he wanted to be and to always remember that "with great power comes great responsibility."

Peter went to Midtown High School and was very focused on getting good grades. He studied hard and got straight As—he loved to learn. Science was Peter's favorite subject, and he was one of the smartest students in class. He enjoyed performing science experiments and showing off his discoveries to his teacher.

After school, Peter worked at the *Daily Bugle* as a photographer. He had a knack for taking pictures—that is, when his boss wasn't yelling at him for more shots of a certain red-and-blue-clad super hero! J. Jonah Jameson, Peter's boss, was known for being tough as nails. He constantly wanted pictures of Spider-Man, but that was a bit of a problem. . . .

Peter had a secret he couldn't tell anyone—not his Aunt May, and certainly not Jameson. He was Spider-Man!

During a school field trip to a lab, a radioactive spider bit Peter! All of a sudden, Peter found he could do extraordinary things like shoot spider webs! At first, he had trouble aiming the webs.

But he used his knowledge of science to make special web-shooters that gave him the control he needed. He kept practicing and, soon enough, he could direct the webs wherever he wanted!

Knowing he had to keep his identity a secret, Peter made himself a spider-suit and a mask fit for a super hero! Now he could go into the city without anyone knowing it was him. He could stick to walls, so he could travel above the streets to stay out of sight when he needed to. Eventually, with time and a lot of practice, Peter learned how to master all of his skills.

Besides web-shooting and wall-clinging, he also had super-strength. This strength, combined with Peter's courage and other powers, gave him the ability to help those in trouble. He made it his mission to protect the people in his neighborhood. That's how he earned the nickname "your friendly neighborhood Spider-Man."

Peter also had the power of
spider-sense. A strong tingling
sensation would alert him to
bad guys and danger.

There was one super villain who was Spider-Man's greatest enemy: Venom! Venom could shape-shift, use his suit to make special weapons, and even mimic Spider-Man's abilities. With his super-strength and menacing fangs, Venom was extremely dangerous. And he loved to wreak havoc in New York City! Spider-Man swung onto the street and fired his webs to stop Venom.

"I'm going to take all of your powers," Venom snarled.

Spider-Man knew Venom well, and knew one of his weaknesses: He hated loud noises! Spider-Man blasted webs at several nearby cars, setting off loud, blaring car alarms!

"What was that, Venom? I can't hear you!" Spider-Man smirked.

Venom was caught completely off guard, giving Spider-Man just enough time to ensnare Venom in thick webbing!

The life of a super hero kept the web-slinger on his toes. Just days later, he surprised the Looter as he was trying to rob a bank.

Thwip! Thwip! Spider-Man shot a series of webs that pinned him down. Then Spider-Man safely returned the stolen money to the authorities.

Spider-Man hoped the day would come when the world would be free from criminals and villains. Until then, he swung through the city on patrol, ready for his spider-sense to alert him to danger, poised to jump in and help wherever he could.

It wasn't easy leading a double life, but he knew he had been given
his powers for a reason. As long as there were bad guys around, he had
an important job to do. Peter Parker was Spider-Man!